Intermedi
(Lord Hear

This little book is dedicated to my family who have frequently led, sometimes driven me to prayer but always kept alive my belief that God is there and listening.

Inter-mediate Prayer

The world is not short of prayer books and humankind is certainly not short of prayers. The production, therefore, of yet another collection should be supported by plausible reasons but I am not sure that, as the author, I can throw very much light on why I put pen to paper for this small offering. Partly it was because, amongst all the disposable prayers that I have composed and managed to use up with a reckless disregard for economy, one or two seemed worth keeping. Enough, it seemed, to make a small anthology to prove that it is within the power of each of us to create our own communications bank with the almighty. If that explanation seems like cloaking pride in good intentions then the next best reason I can offer is that, when I retired, I promised God that the first book I wrote would be a book of prayers.

Why 'inter-mediate'? This is an easier conundrum to explain. I cannot claim to be an advanced petitioner or supplicant. The advanced supplicant is one for whom prayer is an indispensable and comprehensive communion with God. He or she is a votary whose reward is a deep understanding of matters spiritual and perhaps even a mystical experience. They not only make their offering directly to God but receive in kind with varying degrees of certainty. For them prayer is an abiding security and has a continuing purpose whatever the adverse circumstances or trials. They have at their command a whole range of approaches from the 'crie de coeur' to the rich tapestry of beautifying prose and poetry. They cross the threshold of mystery with confidence.

Nor do I consider myself to be a beginner who turns to prayer only in moments of trouble and stress. Beginners call for help in times of urgent need; or, in anger and desperation, they rail against the vicissitudes that befall them. They may also be those for whom the notion of talking to God steals compellingly into their thoughts. They grope for words which will express their feelings, their doubts, their hopes or their religious yearnings. They stand uncertainly at the dawn of spiritual experience but their essays beyond are vulnerable. Too often the flow of spirituality dries up; the complexities of life cloud or extinguish the burgeoning light of understanding.

Somewhere between the votary and the beginner is where I find myself - at the stage of trying hard to mediate a personal relationship with God. In other words, at the 'inter-mediate' stage. And there must be many in similar circumstances. I use the word to convey a broad category which includes all those simple ways of communicating with God, from praise to submission, which meet the everyday needs of ordinary supplicants. Generally intermediates are self-centred seekers. They want to do things their way. They are not lightly deterred by setbacks, or the discovery that the answers to prayers can be capricious; they accept that there seems to be no good reason why some prayers are answered and others not. They have discovered that prayers disperse into a spiritual silence not unlike a pregnant pause in human conversation. Nevertheless they hold to the hope or belief that prayer is somehow 'heard' and that the hearing thereof somehow changes what was into what now is, albeit imperceptibly. And they are determined to continue. They occupy the intermediate position beyond the beginners but not worthy of the intimacy with God accorded to the elect.

Why we pray, where, and how, may be of great importance but I have to confess that, having frequently addressed such questions, I have found no acceptable answers. Consequently, I have taken refuge in the practice of prayer believing that there is greater merit in actually doing it than in indulging in esoteric speculation about it. I suspect I am not alone in this subterfuge. Is there anyone who has not, at some time or other, turned to prayer rather than torment themselves with the philosophical reasons for doing so? Perhaps in a moment of great distress or danger, or at a time of considerable grief or uncontrollable joy? Is there any human condition that has not been prayed about? Prayer is universal and natural like love and awe. Knowing this does not make it any less mysterious but it strengthens the voice of those who pray from the conviction that prayers are heard.

I have found that prayer is best understood by praying: either alone, as a personal matter, or with others as a shared spiritual experience. Although the shared spiritual experience has its own proven worth, the difficulty is that there are so many congregations to join, so many courses to follow, and so many possibilities to consider. This is not a problem for advanced supplicants because for them the spiritual path is well determined and the choices clear. For the intermediates the way may not be so obvious. Of course, they could seek a mentor, pastor or guru, or cultivate the comfort of a denomination but the risk of being deceived is a deterrent. It is disturbing to think that one can be misled by false teachers who claim to be God's elect or to be guardians of the golden key. There are also those, who should know better, who may indeed have the ear of God but who clamour so loudly about it that others, particularly intermediates, and certainly beginners, cannot hear the messages. In the face of the treachery of the first and the trumpeting of the second it is as well to hold fast to the fact that each of us has different needs and a unique spirituality.

There comes a time early in the intermediate's spiritual life when he or she has to seek their own level and 'voice'. It is because I believe level and voice to be fundamental to communicating with God that at present I prefer to pray at the personal level rather than as part of a shared spiritual experience. I find it more telling. To the many who disagree and who enjoy a strong communion with God's people I can only say that, as an intermediate, I am sensitive to the strong possibility that there are no absolutes, no certainties and there will be many false trails. Intermediates have to come to God through simple conversation with Him and I look to prayer to enlighten me in this matter of conversing with God. Later, no doubt, one can pass from sitting by the well of Jericho to being a member of the group.

For the inter-mediate, there are no formalities to be adhered to when trying to make contact with God. Praying can usually be initiated as readily as conversation in whatever place one may find privacy -

Lord I need you to talk to
Now and again
Just quietly
To ask how things are going
And to rehearse my fears and hopes
In my mind I shall expect you to do something:
In my heart I know the decision is yours.

There may be some awkwardness at first but once the effort has been made it can rapidly gather strength, especially if one participant is prepared to listen and the other to go on talking. And God is indisputably the ultimate listener with eternity at his disposal.

The beginning of the day commends itself as prime time for prayers. Not only is it suffused with possibilities and speculation but it also offers the opportunity of renewed life and the chance to grasp the optimistic view -

This is another day
The Lord has made
I rejoice and am pleased with it
May all I do be of his substance
And contribute to his eternal glory.

It provides a space in the day to think of others...

Lord as we open the day's transactions
I commend to you my family [here name].
Grant each your support,
Bestow upon them your blessing and grace
And draw them towards your eternity.

And can be used to focus on the special needs of those dear to us...

There are those dear to us who concern,
Others for whom we have a responsibility
We pray for them
That they too may share the good things
You have bestowed on us.
We would want their problems

To be early resolved
And their prayers more surely achieve, O Lord
Grant that their uncertainties over
Which we have no control
May be settled and their future firmly based.

Not every day dawns to a chorus of joyous expectation and there are bound to be problems ahead, worries and concerns that creep insidiously into one's thoughts ...

Lord, this is likely to be a difficult day.
There will be many things to do
And little time in which to do them.
Some of which lies ahead will need all my tact,
Experience and ability with
which you have endowed me.
When the business of the day predominates
And when there is a pause
In the transactions, nudge me to remember you.

Alternatively there may not be anything particularly worrying in the coming day but one wants to keep in touch ...

Lord, I know that you have things
To say to me today.
Help me to listen through the noisy interference
Of the work-a-day world.
Give me some moments of fruitful silence
To hear your message
And allow me the strength to respond.

Or be reassured that guidance will be forthcoming...

O God who ordered the universe
And everything around me,
So order my affairs today
That they fulfil your purposes.
But also grant me
Sufficient light of revelation
That I can understand
What it is I must do

And sufficient strength of spirit
That I can do it.

Or even to rise above it all...

O Lord, when the daily round has burdens,
Concern for which intrudes upon the day -
Lift me into the sky and let me share the light.

Once the day is under way then it can be fairly safely predicted that it will bring its own assortment of uncertainties to challenge one's belief or understanding...

Lord. Today, I know I will learn again
Of the vicissitudes of life
Of tempests, floods, poverty and of men serving
Cruelty on each other.
And I will want to know why it should be so.
Counsel me in these mysteries and guide my hand
To help where it is needed.
But use my love to serve the stricken.

There will be the problem of knowing whether one is doing the right thing...

Almighty God. I do not know whether
I am pleasing you or not,
And I have no way of telling.

Sometimes the voices in my head tell me one thing
And sometimes another and
I am bewildered by their contradiction.

Help me to listen more closely, more discriminatingly so that I will know
When the voices speak for you, that I may follow that which is right.

Even when we think we know the right thing to do, it is not easy to do it and we need help and reassurance...

Lord, you know I have this problem,
It must seem strange to you,
From where you are and what you know,
That I cannot find a solution,
But I cannot and I need help.
Give me some understanding of what must be done,

Guide me in doing it, and give me persistence
To see it through to resolution.

Sometimes the problem is not so much bewilderment as recognising the solution when it presents itself...

Lord forgive my shortcomings.
I have been asked the questions
But I do not have the wit to find the answers,
Nor the wisdom to understand their significance.
In my ignorance I am as one in a dark place
Who sees shadowy shapes
And surmises what they are.
When the light flashes it is too bright for revelation
And the after images flicker and fade.

Often there is interference from one's own inadequacies which persist and irritate...

O Lord, I do strive to attain the best
But the yoke of mediocrity
Rests heavily on my efforts.
Each finished task bears the blemishes
That come from limited talents.
Allow my shortcomings and
Help me to live with them.
Accept what I do achieve towards
That ultimate perfection
Of which we are all part.

Sometimes the problems are deep and dark...

Dear Lord, I believe I have learned
To cope with the everyday
Sins that are the currency of life and
To trust in your unwavering forgiveness.
But I need help to face the black wickedness
That lurks deep in my heart
And rises uninvited to invade my thoughts.
Help me to acknowledge it is there
And to overcome it,
Have mercy on me and grant me the absolution
That comes out of redemption.

And need forgiveness...

Lord forgive the black wickedness
That lies deep within my heart
And the dark deed,
or shabby thought that marred today.

Sometimes one's inadequacies and misdemeanours assail our confidence or threaten to destabilise our belief...

Now when despair is crumbling
Our hope and confidence away,
Guide us to the firm rock which is your love.
Help us to determine what it is we must do
And strengthen our will to do it,
For we easily weaken and our courage fails.

Or bite deeply into our hope and sap our spirits...

What do I say Lord, what do I do now
That my spirit has been drained by unnecessary anxieties?
How do I refresh and uplift my soul?
I have no source but thee
No hope but thee yet thou art hidden from me.
Allow me one brief glimpse of Truth
And I shall soar where paradise is.

Yet even thus far into harvesting the fruits of human frailty and despair there is hope...

Good Lord; when I am discouraged
By today's problems
And encompassed by doubts,
Be with me to show me some
Light of hope, however faint.
And when the gentle radiance comes
May I reflect it in my words and
Deeds so that others may know,
With me, that life is good.

And doubts can be overcome by insights...

O Lord, we are easily persuaded to doubt,
And will victims of uncertainty,
Seeking signs and proofs.
Help us to accept the insights that are ours
And to proceed in faith for the rest
Recognising that our limitations are human.

Furthermore, when doubts or transgressions seem to bar us from spiritual discourse, it is still open to us to seek reconnection...

> ***O Lord, I have been too long***
> ***In the wilderness of discontent;***
> ***I have wondered with envy and dissatisfaction***
> ***From barren hope to comfortless self pity.***
> ***Let me return to the rich landscape***
> ***Of spiritual and human love.***

Reconnections are more easily managed when we recognise our own insignificance...

> ***Almighty God. It is very difficult for***
> ***Some or us to acknowledge***
> ***Our insignificance and to realise how little***
> ***We organise our lives or control our destiny.***
> ***We often find the burdens laid upon us intolerable***
> ***Or unjust and the tasks which fall to us to be***
> ***Heavy and meaningless.***

Help us to see more clearly with love and charity,
The part that we have to play
In the pattern of events which touch our lives,
And give us inner power to accomplish
That which will have your praise.

Dwelling on one's shortcomings has virtues but it does result in the acute realisation that communication with God can only be very imperfect. In an age when the communication systems between humans is nearing perfection this truth is an aggravation...

O God, if there is a plan I cannot perceive it,
Or any sign of it which makes sense to me.
Perhaps it is right that this should be so.
Perhaps I have no right to know.
But give me some hint, some glimpse
Of the divine purpose
And I will have no need to know.

And the desire for some insights or, better still some degree of certainty, is strong...

Lord, I would settle for one insight,

One glimpse of meaning (In what I do)
If you have a purpose it is not clear to me
And the clamour of the voices which claim to
speak for you is so discordant and confusing
That I cannot hear your message.
I wait patiently for my own voice to enlighten me
But it is silent and I live in lonely uncertainty.

It may be some comfort to reflect that it is not only one's own fragile self-knowledge or lack of ability to formulate a message which is the problem. Nor is it merely human ineptitude where communication is concerned. God is more often obscure than straight forward and his communications to us are generally tantalisingly enigmatic...

Father, why are some things (events)
Ordained to be (come to pass)
Unhindered and others to cause nothing but
trouble?
Why such glorious success, of effortless perfection
For some but not for others?
Why do we have mediocrity and average -
Surely not for the best and superior
To be measured against?
These are questions I cannot find answers for.
I need to know If I am to continue as one and not
Another.

To such an extent that our desire to understand can reach the point of being desperate...

> ***O God! tell me why and let me glimpse***
> ***Some part of the secret of life.***
> ***As it is I grapple with the complexities of each day,***
> ***The fluctuations from joy to sadness,***
> ***From hope to despair, and the frustrations***
> ***Of human miconsistancies -***
> ***Like a blind man seeking to know his space.***
> ***Why God, why?***

Yet, given our own inherently pathetic inadequacy, the threadbare nature of our contacts with God have to be understood...

> ***Father, you have created your mysteries***
> ***Too well for my understanding.***
> ***I see them but as one of a host,***
> ***Honoured by the participation but***

Bewildered by the magnitude.
Reassure me that it all has meaning in you.

One blessing, which emerges from submission to reality, is that it contains the seeds of salvation...

Lord, I know that I am weak and insignificant
For all around me is evidence of the
Vastness and power of creation.
Yet I nourish the belief that I,
Unimportant as I am,
May enjoy salvation and answers to my prayers.
But attend sympathetically to my needs
And the needs of my family and I shall be happy.

On the other hand it does not hurt to remind God, omnipotence apart, that we have a voice...

Lord I want to register with you
What you already know
Because I need to be assured

My prayer has been dispatched.
O Lord, who has the power to turn
Mountains into seas
And seas into mountains, to create new galaxies
Or destroy failing suns....
Do not ignore me because I have petty needs.

Curiously it is the omnipotence of the almighty that creates some measure of disconnection. Why do we bother to pray when apparently what we wish to say is known even before we say it...

Lord you know everything
Why do I need to say anything ?

On the other hand, when praying into what appears to be a vacuum, there are benefits in stressing that the messages have been sent...

Lord I want to register with you
What you already know
Because I need to know
My prayer has been dispatched.

The knowledge that God knows a thing or two can be an advantage when communication is difficult and when, struggle as we might, the words just will not come...

Lord, I rely on you to understand what it is
That I am trying to say in case the inadequacies of my worries and the frailty of my self-knowledge
Should obscure my message.

Amidst all this preoccupation-occupation with one-self, which is the hallmark of the intermediate, it is as well to remember that almost everyone else's plight is worse than our own. It is important to the development of one's spiritual understanding and will help to take us beyond the present stage. It is also important in its own right and one should make times during the day when the needs of others can be addressed strongly...

There are millions of people worse off than me,
Lord, and yet knowing this I still
Bemoan my own condition.
Lead me to understand the sufferings of others
And teach me what I must do to help.

Even given such altruism the intermediate should not be surprised if his or her own pre-occupations creep back...

O Lord, what right have I to bring my problems
When the rest of the world has
So many more pressing ones?
Yet if I am to cope with today I must
Share my concerns with you -
Burden you with some of more urgent
Anxieties and worries.
Bear with me, be near me and see me through.

If remembering the adversities of others is necessary for spiritual growth, then meditation and reflection and even reverie are equally significant...

Be still...
Where the rhythms are broader and deeper
Than the world acknowledges;
Listen...
Beyond the sounds that clutter the day;
Look...
At the light and not at the things that it settles on;
Touch...
Nothing but that it reminds you of your humanity;
Wait...
Where the prayers are.

Opportunities to subjugate the tawdry transactions of the day need to be grasped firmly and enjoyed...

Grant me O God

Time to stay where the bird's sing
To pause where silent sun
Filters through the woodland shade -
And time to sigh.

And the chance to step aside from the flow of the day sought rigorously...

Father, so much slips away
Obscured by the churlish demands of the daily round,
And so much surrenders to less worthy attentions.
Lift aside the veil so that I can appreciate you gifts,
Breathe the deep significance of moments of harmony;
Sink into each moment of peace,
And live in the beautiful.

Such moments have to be harvested...

Lord, help me to gather today's precious moments,
Especially the moment of perceived beauty,
Of fleeting joy and satisfied duty,
Of shared devotion and loyalty
And the wealth of the ordinary.

Eventually, there will come a time when some prayer, some part of a prayer or maybe just the humour of a prayer, will be answered. The joy will be boundless...

Father this is the fulfilment of a hope;
A gift of which I am not worthy.
Please trust me to make the most of it and
Grant me the joy of doing it well.

With the joy, and no doubt the relief that prayer is not all input and little outcome, will come the desire to make a positive response. Some show of gratitude seems the right thing to do, but what...

Lord, how can I say thank you
Except in small human ways?
By offering hope and encouragement
Where damning words might choose to come;
By giving love where indifference would be easy,
By fielding faith where fear would hope to reign
And by embracing all whom I meet today
With the warmth of your grace.
Doing all things well in the glare of the night.

If the start of the day is the prime time for praying the preparatory prayers, then the end of the day has its place as the time to pull together the events that have gone before.

> ***Lord, I am glad to have had today.***
> ***Help me to bring it to a close in quiet gratitude***

And try to assess performance...

> ***Lord, the day is over***
> ***And what is done cannot be undone.***
> ***Credit me with that which has pleased you***
> ***And forgive me for that which has not.***

Inevitably assessing performance leads to the painful identification of limitations...

> ***Lord as I approach the end of this week,***

I offer to you what little I have achieved.
I have made no significant contribution to world events,
Made no major discoveries
And made little progress towards enlightenment.
But I am reassured that you will recognise
The worth of what I have done.

Whatever the time of day, however, it is salutary to remind oneself that we manage little of our own life...

I am in your hands Lord
(Was it ever any other way no matter how much I pretend)
Treat me with compassion
And test me only so far as you know I can endure.

Finally, a lifetime is not much, no matter how long it

may be, and one is mindful of just how much there is to do and how little time we are given to do it in. There is no harm in pleading for an extension...

Lord, I know my death must come to pass
But may I ask this gift of you -
Not today, when I've work to do
But if now is the chosen time
Excuse me please for more than some
Of all the things I've left undone.

I have no doubt, from experience, of the value of creating a personal prayer. For something with a special meaning we often have to rely on our own words. We make do with the day-to-day idioms and vulgar expressions that constitute the common discourse. Their virtue is that they chime with our own times and our own understanding. Happily, from God's point of view, no doubt, the message and the intention are what count and we should not be reticent about expressing what we have to say in our own way. It is important that we have opportunities to say what is within us and not to rely only on the words of others to carry our spiritual baggage. If, by careful crafting, we can make each prayer elegant, or shapely and if we can also make it brief yet encompassing all that we want to say, then it has the added virtue of being pleasing in its own right. This is not as difficult as it may seem. I have found that the need generates the prayer, the moment calls the words. Given encouragement they come tumbling into consciousness and plead to be twisted gently into shape. It can be done in the most unpromising places : on the train, standing on a station, walking along the road, in the bath. It is a discipline that in time shapes the message and hones the communication. Well done it has resonances which reverberate through the silence which follows and even badly done it has its own spiritual value that cannot be reckoned.

I also have no doubt that the level of personal prayer exercised in this collection,, when allowed to predominate, becomes a self indulgence and no longer trades in its special mystery. It is not realistic to imagine that, every time we need to pray, our own words are the only words. It is not given to us to create beautiful and significant prose every day and there will be times when we do not easily conjure the words that convey most effectively what we have to say. In such circumstances the condition of the commonplace is no longer satisfactory and it becomes clear that a possible major defect of the personal prayer is that it lacks any sense of true contemplation. Coming as it does from within, and being part of its creator, it is limited. It is at such moments that the words of others have to be recruited.

When that possibility is faced, one is, I suspect, standing at the culmination of the intermediate's achievement. Exactly how progression from this point on is achieved lies outside the scope of this book. Collections are legion, as any brief search in the nave of a church or religious bookshop will show. The reader will have no difficulty finding something to suit but before signing off it may be worth just remembering the fulcrum of Christian prayer - The Lord's Prayer. It is not surprising that it has been called into service for all manner of purposes often when no other words commend or suggest themselves. It is because it says so much in so few words that it is a benchmark for any good prayer.

Our Father which art in heaven
Hallowed be thy name
Thy kingdom come
Thy will be done
On earth as it is in heaven
Give us this day our daily bread
Forgive us our trespasses

As we forgive those who trespass against us
Lead us not into temptation
Deliver us from evil
For thine is the Kingdom
The Power and the Glory
Forever and ever
Amen.

It has another virtue for the intermediate's next stage because it is like all well honed prayers, especially those from the older and accredited texts: it is open to interpretation. The language is creative and encourages and enables a range of interpretations to be made so that each individual supplicant's special needs are met. Such language can plumb depths and tap needs the supplicant did not know about. It's great virtue and strength are, in my view, that it is contemplative and can be dwelt upon with great rewards. By comparison, modern speech may be more direct but it is utilitarian and lacks connections. As intermediates we are, indeed, fortunate. There is a wealth of prayer to quarry and use alongside our own humble, but equally valuable, contribution.

D A Denegri
December 1994

Edited by Jane Eaglesome
www.pauldenegripandon.com

Printed in Great Britain
by Amazon

64589877R10020